HORRID HENRY

FUN IN THE SUN

FRANCESCA SIMON

ILLUSTRATED BY TONY ROSS

Orion

ORION CHILDREN'S BOOKS

Stories first published in "Horrid Henry Gets Rich Quick", "Horrid Henry",
"Horrid Henry and the Mega-Mean Time Machine", "Horrid Henry and the
Football Fiend", "Horrid Henry and the Bogey Babysitter" and
"Horrid Henry and the Mummy's Curse" respectively.

This collection first published in Great Britain in 2019 by Hodder and Stoughton

1 3 5 7 9 10 8 6 4 2

Text © Francesca Simon, 1998, 1994, 2004, 2006, 2002, 2000
Illustrations © Tony Ross, 1998, 1994, 2004, 2006, 2002, 2000
Puzzles and activities © Orion Children's Books 2019
Additional images © Shutterstock

A CIP catalogue record for this book is available from the British Library.

ISBN 978 1 51010 618 5

Printed and bound in Great Britain by Clays Ltd, Elcograf S.p.A

The paper and board used in this book are from well-managed
forests and other responsible sources.

Orion Children's Books
An imprint of
Hachette Children's Group
Part of Hodder and Stoughton
Carmelite House
50 Victoria Embankment
London EC4Y 0DZ

An Hachette UK Company
www.hachette.co.uk
www.hachettechildrens.co.uk
www.horridhenry.co.uk

HORRID HENRY

FUN IN THE SUN

FRANCESCA SIMON

FRANCESCA SIMON SPENT HER CHILDHOOD ON THE BEACH IN CALIFORNIA AND STARTED WRITING STORIES AT THE AGE OF EIGHT. SHE WROTE HER FIRST HORRID HENRY BOOK IN 1994. HORRID HENRY HAS GONE ON TO CONQUER THE GLOBE; HIS ADVENTURES HAVE SOLD MILLIONS OF COPIES WORLDWIDE.

FRANCESCA HAS WON THE CHILDREN'S BOOK OF THE YEAR AWARD AND IN 2009 WAS AWARDED A GOLD BLUE PETER BADGE. SHE WAS ALSO A TRUSTEE OF THE WORLD BOOK DAY CHARITY FOR SIX YEARS.

FRANCESCA LIVES IN NORTH LONDON WITH HER FAMILY.

WWW.FRANCESCASIMON.COM WWW.HORRIDHENRY.CO.UK @SIMON_FRANCESCA

TONY ROSS

TONY ROSS WAS BORN IN LONDON AND STUDIED AT THE LIVERPOOL SCHOOL OF ART AND DESIGN. HE HAS WORKED AS A CARTOONIST, A GRAPHIC DESIGNER, AN ADVERTISING ART DIRECTOR AND A UNIVERSITY LECTURER.

TONY IS ONE OF THE MOST POPULAR AND SUCCESSFUL CHILDREN'S ILLUSTRATORS OF ALL TIME, BEST KNOWN FOR ILLUSTRATING HORRID HENRY AND THE WORKS OF DAVID WALLIAMS, AS WELL AS HIS OWN HUGELY POPULAR SERIES, THE LITTLE PRINCESS. HE LIVES IN MACCLESFIELD.

CONTENTS

HORRID HENRY'S
SPORTS DAY

"We all want sports day to be a great success tomorrow," announced Miss Battle-Axe. "I am here to make sure that *no one*" – she glared at Horrid Henry – "**SPOILS** it."

Horrid Henry glared back. Horrid Henry hated sports day. Last year he hadn't won a single event. He'd **dropped** his egg in the egg-and-spoon race, **TRIPPED** over Rude Ralph in the three-legged race, and **collided** with Sour Susan in the sack race. Henry's team had even lost the tug-of-war.

9

Most sickening of all, Perfect Peter had won *both* his races.

If only the school had a sensible day, like TV-watching day, or chocolate-eating day, or who could guzzle the most crisps day, **Horrid Henry** would be sure to win every prize. But no. *He* had to *leap* and *dash* about getting hot and bothered in front of stupid parents. When he became king he'd make teachers run all the races then behead the winners. KING HENRY THE HORRIBLE grinned happily.

"Pay attention, Henry!" barked Miss

Battle-Axe. "What did I just say?"

Henry had no idea. "Sports day is cancelled?" he suggested hopefully.

Miss Battle-Axe fixed him with her steely eyes. "I said no one is to bring any sweets tomorrow. You'll all be given a delicious, refreshing piece of orange."

Henry slumped in his chair, SCOWLING. All he could do was hope for rain.

Sports day dawned bright and sunny.

RATS, thought Henry. He could, of course, pretend to be sick. But he'd tried that last year and Mum hadn't been **FOOLED**. The year before that he'd complained he'd hurt his leg. Unfortunately Dad then caught him *dancing* on the table.

It was no use. He'd just have to take part. If only he could win a race!

Perfect Peter **BOUNCED** into his room.

"Sports day today!" beamed Peter. "And *I'm* responsible for bringing the hard-boiled **eggs** for the egg-and-spoon races. Isn't it exciting!"

"**NO!**" screeched Henry. "Get out of here!"

"But I only . . ." began Peter.

Henry *leapt* at him, **roaring**. He was a cowboy lassoing a runaway steer.

"**EEEAAARGH!**" SQUEALED Peter.

"Stop being **HORRID**, Henry!" shouted Dad. "Or no pocket money this week!"

Henry let Peter go.

"It's so unfair," he muttered, picking up his clothes from the floor and putting them on. Why did he never win?

Henry reached under his bed and filled his pockets from the secret sweet tin he kept there. **Horrid Henry** was a **master** at eating sweets in school without being detected. At least he could scoff something good while the others were **STUCK** eating dried-up old orange pieces.

Then he **stomped** downstairs. Perfect Peter was busy packing hard-boiled eggs into a carton.

Horrid Henry sat down **SCOWLING** and gobbled his breakfast.

"Good luck, boys," said Mum. "I'll be there to cheer for you."

"**Humph,**" growled Henry.

"Thanks, Mum," said Peter. "I expect I'll w**i**n my egg-and-spoon race again but of course it doesn't matter if I don't. It's how you play that counts."

"**SHUT UP, PETER!**" snarled Henry. Egg-and-spoon! Egg-and-spoon!

15

If Henry heard that **DISGUSTING** phrase once more he would start **FROTHING** at the mouth.

"Mum! Henry told me to shut up," WAILED Peter, "and he **ATTACKED** me this morning."

"Stop being **HORRID**, Henry," said Mum. "Peter, come with me and we'll comb your hair. I want you to look your best when you win that trophy again."

Henry's blood boiled. He felt like *snatching* those eggs and *hurling* them against the wall.

16

Then Henry had a wonderful, SPECTACULAR idea. It was so wonderful that . . . Henry heard Mum coming back down the stairs. There was no time to lose crowing about his brilliance.

Horrid Henry *ran* to the fridge, grabbed another egg carton and SWAPPED it for the box of hard-boiled ones on the counter.

"Don't forget your eggs, Peter," said Mum. She handed the carton to Peter, who tucked it safely in his school bag.

Tee hee, thought Horrid Henry.

Henry's class lined up on the playing fields. **FLASH!** A small figure wearing gleaming white trainers *zipped* by. It was Aerobic Al, the fastest boy in Henry's class.

"Gotta run, gotta run, gotta run,"

he chanted, gliding into place beside
Henry. "I will, of course, win every
event," he announced. "I've been
training all year. My dad's got a *special*
place all ready for my trophies."

"Who wants to race anyway?"
SNEERED Horrid Henry, sneaking
a **yummy gummy fuzzball** into
his mouth.

"Now, teams for the three-legged
race," **BARKED** Miss Battle-Axe
into her megaphone. "This is a race
showing how well you co-operate and
use teamwork with your partner.

Ralph will race with William, Josh will race with Clare, Henry . . ." she glanced at her list, ". . . you will race with Margaret."

"**NO!**" screamed Horrid Henry.

"**NO!**" screamed Moody Margaret.

"**YES**," said Miss Battle-Axe.

"But I want to be with Susan," said Margaret.

"No fussing," said Miss Battle-Axe. "Bert, where's your partner?"

"I dunno," said Beefy Bert.

Henry and Margaret stood as far apart as possible while their legs

20

were tied together.

"You'd better do as I say, Henry," HISSED Margaret. "*I'll* decide how we race."

"*I* will, you mean," HISSED Henry.

"**READY . . . STEADY . . . GO!**"

Miss Battle-Axe blew her whistle.

They were off! Henry moved to the left, Margaret moved to the right.

"**THIS WAY, HENRY!**" shouted Margaret. She tried to drag him.

"**No, this way!**" shouted Henry. He tried to drag her.

They *lurched* wildly, left and right, then **toppled** over.

CRASH! Aerobic Al and Lazy Linda tripped over the **SCREAMING** Henry and Margaret.

SMASH! Rude Ralph and Weepy William fell over Al and Linda.

BUMP! Dizzy Dave and Beefy Bert collided with Ralph and William.

"**WAAA!**" wailed Weepy William.

"It's all your fault, Margaret!" shouted Henry, pulling her hair.

"No, yours," shouted Margaret, pulling his harder.

Miss Battle-Axe blew her whistle frantically.

"**STOP! STOP!**" she ordered. "Henry! Margaret! What an example to set for the younger ones. Any more nonsense like that and you'll be severely punished. Everyone, get ready for the **EGG-AND-SPOON** race!"

This was it! The moment Henry

had been waiting for.

The children lined up in their teams. Moody Margaret, Sour Susan and Anxious Andrew were going first in Henry's class. Henry glanced at Peter.

Yes, there he was, *smiling* proudly, next to Goody-Goody Gordon, Spotless

Sam and Tidy Ted. The eggs lay still
on their spoons. Horrid Henry held
his breath.

"**READY . . . STEADY . . . GO!**"

shouted Miss Battle-Axe.

They were off!

"Go, Peter, go!" shouted Mum.

Peter walked *faster* and *faster* and
faster. He was in the lead. He was
pulling away from the field. Then
. . . **wobble** . . . **wobble** . . . SPLAT!

"**AAAAAGH!**" yelped Peter.

Moody Margaret's egg wobbled.

Then Susan's.

SPLAT!

Then everybody's.

SPLAT!

SPLAT!

SPLAT!

"I've got egg on my shoes!" wailed Margaret.

"I've ruined my new dress!" SHRIEKED Susan.

"I've got egg all over me!" SQUEALED Tidy Ted.

"Help!" squeaked Perfect Peter. Egg dripped down his trousers.

Parents surged forward, screaming and waving handkerchiefs and towels.

Rude Ralph and Horrid Henry SHRIEKED with laughter.

Miss Battle-Axe blew her whistle.

"Who brought the **eggs?**" asked Miss Battle-Axe. Her voice was like ice.

"I did," said Perfect Peter. "But I brought hard-boiled ones."

"OUT!" shouted Miss Battle-Axe.

"Out of the games!"

"But . . . but . . ." gasped Perfect Peter.

"No buts, out!" She glared. "Go straight to the Head."

Perfect Peter **burst** into tears and crept away.

Horrid Henry could hardly contain himself. This was the **BEST** sports day he'd ever been to.

"The rest of you, stop laughing at once. Parents, get back to your seats! Time for the next race!" ordered Miss Battle-Axe.

28

All things considered, thought **Horrid Henry**, lining up with his class, it hadn't been too **TERRIBLE** a day. He'd loved the egg-and-spoon race, of course. And he'd had **FUN** *pulling* the other team into a muddy puddle in the tug-of-war, knocking over the obstacles in the obstacle race, and **crashing** into Aerobic Al in the sack race.

But, oh, to actually win something!

There was just one race left before sports day was over. The cross-country run. The event Henry **HATED** more than any other. One long, sweaty, **EXHAUSTING** lap round the whole field.

Henry heaved his heavy bones to the starting line. His final chance to win . . . yet he knew there was no hope. If he beat Weepy William he'd be doing well.

Suddenly Henry had a wonderful, **SPECTACULAR IDEA**. Why

30

had he never thought of this before? Truly, he was a genius. Wasn't there some ancient Greek who'd won a race by throwing down golden apples which his rival kept stopping to pick up? Couldn't he, Henry, learn something from those old Greeks?

"**READY** . . . **STEADY** . . . **GO!**" shrieked Miss Battle-Axe.

Off they *dashed*.

"Go, Al, go!" yelled his father.

"Get a move on, Margaret!" **SHRIEKED** her mother.

"Go, Ralph!" cheered his father.

31

"Do your best, Henry," said Mum.

Horrid Henry reached into his pocket and hurled some sweets. They **THUDDED** to the ground in front of the runners.

"Look, sweets!" shouted Henry.

Al checked behind him. He was well in the lead. He paused and scooped up one sweet, and then another. He glanced behind again, then started unwrapping the **yummy gummy fuzzball**.

"Sweets!" yelped Greedy Graham. He stopped to pick up as many as he could find then stuffed them in his mouth.

"*YUMMY!*" screamed Graham.

"*Sweets!* Where?" chanted the others. Then they stopped to look.

"Over there!" yelled Henry, throwing another handful. The racers paused to *pounce* on the treats.

While the others **MUNCHED** and **CRUNCHED**, Henry made a frantic dash for the lead.

He was out in front! Henry's legs moved as they had never moved before, pounding round the field. And there was the finishing line!

THUD! THUD! THUD!

Henry glanced back. Oh no! Aerobic Al was catching up!

Henry felt in his pocket. He had one **GIANT** gob-stopper left. He looked round, panting.

"Go home and take a nap, Henry!"

shouted Al, sticking out his tongue as he raced past.

Henry threw down the gob-stopper in front of Al. Aerobic Al hesitated, then *skidded* to a halt and picked it up. He could beat Henry any day so why not show off a bit?

Suddenly Henry *sprinted* past. Aerobic Al dashed after him. **Harder** and **harder**, *faster* and *faster* Henry ran. He was a bird. He was a plane. He flew across the finishing line.

"The winner is . . . Henry?" squeaked Miss Battle-Axe.

"I'VE BEEN ROBBED!"

screamed Aerobic Al.

"HURRAY!" yelled Henry.

Wow, what a great day, thought

Horrid Henry, proudly carrying home

his trophy. Al's dad shouting at Miss Battle-Axe and Mum. Miss Battle-Axe and Mum shouting back. Peter sent off in DISGRACE. And he, Henry, the big winner.

"I can't think how you got those eggs muddled up," said Mum.

"Me neither," said Perfect Peter, SNIFFLING.

"Never mind, Peter," said Henry brightly. "It's not winning, it's *how you play* that counts."

HORRID HENRY'S

HOLIDAY

Horrid Henry hated holidays.

Henry's idea of a SUPER holiday was sitting on the sofa eating **crisps** and watching **TV**.

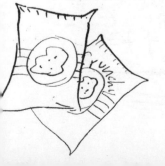

Unfortunately, his parents usually had other plans.

Once they took him to see some castles. But there were no castles.

There were only piles of stones and broken walls.

"Never again," said Henry.

The next year he had to go to a lot of museums.

"Never again," said Mum and Dad.

Last year they went to the seaside.

"The sun is too **HOT**," Henry whined.

"The water is too cold,"
Henry whinged.

"The food is γuckγ," Henry grumbled.

"The bed is **lumpy**," Henry moaned.

This year they decided to try something different.

"We're going camping in France," said Henry's parents.

"**HOORAY!**" said Henry.

"You're happy, Henry?" said Mum. Henry had never been happy about any holiday plans before.

"Oh yes," said Henry. Finally, finally, they were doing something good.

Henry knew all about camping from Moody Margaret. Margaret had been camping with her family.

They had stayed in a big tent with *comfy beds*, a *fridge*, a *cooker*, a *loo*, a *shower*, a *heated swimming pool*, a *disco*, and a *great big giant TV with fifty- seven channels*.

"Oh boy!" said Horrid Henry.

"Bonjour!" said Perfect Peter.

The great day arrived at last.
Horrid Henry, Perfect Peter, Mum
and Dad boarded the ferry for
France.

Henry and Peter had never been
on a boat before.

Henry jumped on and off the seats.

Peter did a lovely drawing.

The boat went UP and DOWN
and UP and DOWN.

Henry ran back and forth between the aisles.

Peter pasted stickers in his notebook.

The boat went UP and DOWN and UP and DOWN.

Henry sat on a revolving chair and spun round.

Peter played with his puppets.

The boat went UP and DOWN and UP and DOWN.

Then Henry and Peter ate a big greasy lunch of sausages and chips in the café.

The boat went UP and DOWN,

and UP and DOWN,

and UP and DOWN.

Henry began to feel queasy.

Peter began to feel queasy.

Henry's face went green.

Peter's face went green.

"I think I'm going to be SICK," said Henry, and threw up all over Mum.

48

"I think I'm going to be—" said Peter, and threw up all over Dad.

"Oh no," said Mum.

"Never mind," said Dad. "I just know this will be our best holiday ever."

Finally, the boat arrived in France. After driving and driving and driving they reached the campsite.

It was even better than Henry's dreams. The tents were as big as houses. Henry heard the happy sound of TVs blaring, music

playing, and children splashing and shrieking. The sun shone. The sky was blue.

"**WOW**, this looks great," said Henry. But the car drove on.

"**STOP!**" said Henry. "You've gone too far."

"We're not staying in that **AWFUL** place," said Dad.

They drove on.

"Here's our campsite," said Dad. "A *real* campsite!"

Henry stared at the bare rocky ground under the *cloudy* grey sky.

There were three small tents flapping
in the wind. There was a single tap.
There were a few trees. There was
NOTHING ELSE.

"It's wonderful!" said Mum.

"It's wonderful!" said Peter.

"But where's the TV?" said Henry.

"No TV here, thank goodness,"
said Mum. "We've got books."

"But where are the **beds?**"
said Henry.

"No beds here, thank goodness,"
said Dad. "We've got sleeping bags."

"But where's the pool?" said Henry.

"No pool," said Dad. "We'll swim
in the river."

"Where's the toilet?" said Peter.

Dad pointed at a distant cubicle.
Three people stood waiting "All the
way over there?" said Peter. "I'm not
complaining" he added quickly.

Mum and Dad unpacked the car.
Henry stood and scowled.

"Who wants to help put up the tent?" asked Mum.

"I do!" said Dad.

"I do!" said Peter.

Henry was horrified. "WE HAVE TO PUT UP OUR OWN TENT?"

"Of course," said Mum.

"I don't like it here," said Henry. "I want to go camping in the other place."

"That's not camping," said Dad. "Those tents have *beds* in them. And *loos*. And *showers*. And *fridges*. And *cookers*, and *TVs*. **Horrible**." Dad shuddered.

"Horrible," said Peter.

"And we have such a **lovely snug** tent here," said Mum. "Nothing modern — just wooden pegs and poles."

"Well, I want to stay there," said Henry.

"We're staying here," said Dad.

"**NO!**" screamed Henry.

"**YES!**" screamed Dad.

I am sorry to say that Henry then had the *LONGEST*, **LOUDEST**, noisiest, shrillest, most **HORRIBLE** tantrum you can imagine.

Did you think that a **horrid** boy like Henry would like nothing better then sleeping on hard rocky

ground
in a soggy
sleeping bag
without a pillow?

   You thought
wrong.

   Henry liked
comfy beds.

   Henry liked CRISP SHEETS.

   Henry liked hot baths.

   Henry liked *microwave dinners*,
TV, and NOISE.

   He did not like cold showers, **fresh
air**, and quiet.

Far off in the distance the sweet sound of loud music drifted towards them.

"Aren't you glad we're not staying in that **AWFUL** noisy place?" said Dad.

"Oh yes," said Mum.

"Oh yes," said Perfect Peter.

Henry pretended he was a bulldozer come to knock down tents and squash campers.

"Henry, don't barge the tent!" yelled Dad.

Henry pretended he was a hungry *Tyrannosaurus Rex*.

"**OW!**" shrieked Peter.

"**Henry, don't be horrid!**"
yelled Mum.

She looked up at the dark *cloudy*
sky.

"It's going to rain," said Mum.

"Don't worry," said Dad. "It
never rains when I'm camping."

"The boys and I will go and collect
some more firewood," said Mum.

"I'm not moving," said
Horrid Henry.

While Dad made a campfire,
Henry played his boom-box
as loud as he could,

stomping in time to the terrible music of the Killer Boy Rats.

"Henry, turn that noise down this minute," said Dad.

Henry pretended not to hear.

"**HENRY!**" yelled Dad.

"*TURN THAT DOWN!*"

Henry turned the volume down the teeniest tiniest fraction.

The **TERRIBLE** sounds of the Killer Boy Rats continued to **BOOM** over the quiet campsite.

Campers emerged from their tents and shook their fists. Dad switched off Henry's tape player.

"Anything wrong, Dad?" asked Henry, in his sweetest voice.

"No," said Dad.

Mum and Peter returned carrying armfuls of firewood.

It started to *drizzle*.

"This is fun," said Mum, slapping a mosquito.

"Isn't it?" said Dad. He was heating up some tins of baked beans.

The *drizzle* turned into a **DOWNPOUR**.

The *wind* blew. The campfire hissed, and went out.

"Never mind," said Dad brightly. "We'll eat our baked beans cold."

Mum was *snoring*.

Dad was *snoring*.

Peter was *snoring*.

Henry tossed and turned. But
whichever way he turned in his
damp sleeping bag, he seemed to be
lying on sharp, pointy stones.

Above him, mosquitoes whined.

I'll never get to sleep, he thought,
kicking Peter.

How am I going to bear this for
fourteen days?

Around four o'clock on Day Five
the family huddled inside the **COLD,
DAMP, SMELLY** tent listening to the
howling wind and the pouring rain.

"Time for a walk!" said Dad.

"**Great idea!**" said Mum, sneezing. "I'll get the boots."

"**Great idea!**" said Peter, sneezing. "I'll get the macs."

"But it's pouring outside," said Henry.

"So?" said Dad. "What better time to go for a walk?"

"I'm not coming," said Horrid Henry.

"I am," said Perfect Peter. "I don't mind the rain."

Dad poked his head outside the tent.

"The rain has stopped," he said.
"I'll remake the fire.

"I'm not coming," said Henry.

"We need more firewood," said
Dad. "Henry can stay here and collect
some. And make sure it's dry."

Henry poked his head outside the
tent. The rain had stopped, but the
sky was still cloudy. The fire spat.

I won't go, thought Henry. The
forest will be all MUDDY and wet.

He looked round to see if there was
any wood closer to home.

That was when he saw the thick,

dry wooden pegs holding up all the tents.

Henry looked to the left.

Henry looked to the right.

No one was around.

If I just take a few pegs from each tent, he thought, they'll never be missed.

When Mum and Dad came back
they were delighted.

"What a lovely roaring fire," said
Mum.

"Clever you to find some dry
wood," said Dad.

The wind blew.

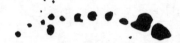

Henry dreamed he was **floating** in
a cold river.

Floating, **floating**, **floating**.

He woke up. He shook his head.
He **was floating**. The tent was filled
with cold muddy water.

Then the tent **collapsed** on top of them.

Henry, Peter, Mum and Dad stood outside in the rain and stared at the river of water gushing through their collapsed tent.

All round them soaking wet campers were staring at their collapsed tents.

Peter Sneezed.

Mum Sneezed.

Dad Sneezed.

Henry coughed, CHOKED, SPLUTTERED and SNEEZED.

"I don't understand it," said Dad.

"This tent *never* collapses."

"What are we going to do?" said
Mum.

"I know," said Henry. "I've got a
very good idea."

Two hours later Mum, Dad, Henry
and Peter were sitting on a sofa-
bed inside a tent as big as a house,
eating CRISPS and watching TV.

The sun was shining. The sky
was blue.

"Now this is what I call a
holiday!" said Henry.

HORRID HENRY'S
HIKE

Horrid Henry looked out of the window. AAAARRRGGGHHH! It was a lovely day. The sun was shining. The birds were tweeting. The breeze was blowing. Little fluffy clouds floated by in a bright blue sky.

RATS.

Why couldn't it be RAINING? Or hailing? Or *sleeting*?

Any minute, any second, it would happen . . . the words he'd been dreading, the words he'd give anything not to hear, the words —

"Henry! Peter! Time to go for a **WALK**," called Mum.

"Yippee!" said Perfect Peter. "I can wear my new yellow wellies!"

"**NO!**" screamed Horrid Henry.

Go for a walk! Go for a walk! Didn't he walk enough already? He walked to school. He walked home from school. He walked to the TV. He walked to the computer. He walked to the sweet jar and all the way back to the comfy black chair. **Horrid Henry** walked plenty. **Ugghh**. The last thing he needed was more walking. More

chocolate, yes. More **CRISPS**, yes.
More *walking*? No way! Why oh why
couldn't his parents ever say, "Henry!
Time to play on the computer." Or
"Henry, **STOP** doing your homework
this minute! Time to turn on the **TV**."

But no. For some reason his **mean**,
HORRIBLE parents thought he spent
too much time sitting indoors. They'd

been threatening for weeks to make him go on a family walk. Now the DREADFUL moment had come. His precious weekend was ruined.

Horrid Henry **HATED** nature. Horrid Henry **HATED** fresh air. What could be more boring than walking up and down streets staring at lamp posts? Or sloshing across some stupid MUDDY park? Nature smelled. UGGH! He'd much rather be inside watching TV.

Mum stomped into the sitting room.

"Henry! Didn't you hear me calling?"

"No," lied Henry.

"Get your wellies on, we're going," said Dad, rubbing his hands. "What a *lovely* day."

"I don't want to go for a walk," said Henry. "I want to watch Rapper Zapper Zaps **Terminator Gladiator**."

"But Henry," said Perfect Peter, "*fresh air* and *exercise* are so good for you."

"**I don't care!**" shrieked Henry.

Horrid Henry stomped downstairs and *flung* open the front door. He breathed in deeply, **HOPPED** on one foot, then shut the door.

"There! Done it. Fresh air and exercise," snarled Henry.

"Henry, we're going," said Mum. "Get in the car."

Henry's ears pricked up.

"The car?" said Henry. "I thought we were going for a walk."

"We are," said Mum. "In the countryside."

"Hurray!" said Perfect Peter. "A nice long walk."

"NOOOO!" howled Henry. Plodding along in the boring old park was bad enough, with its mouldy leaves and

DOG POO and stumpy trees. But at least the park wasn't very big. But the countryside?

The countryside was **enormous!** They'd be walking for hours, days, weeks, months, till his legs wore down to stumps and his feet **fell off**. And the countryside was so **dangerous!** Horrid Henry was sure he'd be **swallowed** up by quicksand or **TRAMPLED** to death by marauding chickens.

"I live in the city!" shrieked Henry. "I don't want to go to the country!"

"Time you got out more," said Dad.

"But look at those clouds," moaned Henry, pointing to a 𝒻𝓁𝓊𝒻𝒻𝓎 wisp. "We'll get **soaked**."

"A little water never hurt anyone," said Mum.

Oh yeah? Wouldn't they be sorry when he died of PNEUMONIA.

"I'M STAYING HERE AND THAT'S FINAL!" screamed Henry.

"Henry, we're waiting," said Mum.

"Good," said Henry.

"I'm all ready, Mum," said Peter.

"I'm going to start deducting pocket money," said Dad. "5p, 10p, 15p, 20—"

Horrid Henry pulled on his wellies, stomped out of the door and got in the car. He **SLAMMED** the door as hard as he could. It was so unfair! Why did he never get to do what he wanted to do? Now he would miss the first time **Rapper Zapper** had ever slugged it out with **Terminator Gladiator**. And all because he had to go on a long, boring, exhausting, **HORRIBLE** hike. He was so miserable he didn't even have the energy to kick Peter.

"Can't we just walk round the block?" moaned Henry.

"N-O spells no," said Dad. "We're going for a lovely walk in the countryside and that's that."

Horrid Henry **slumped** miserably in his seat. Boy would they be sorry when he was **gobbled** up by goats. **Boo Hoo**, if only we hadn't gone on that walk in the wilds, Mum would wail.

Henry was right, we should have listened to him, Dad would **SOB**. I miss Henry, Peter would **howl**. I'll never eat goat's cheese again. And now it's too late, they would **SHRIEK**.

If only, thought Horrid Henry. That would serve them right.

All too soon, Mum pulled into a carpark on the edge of a small wood.

"**Wow**," said Perfect Peter. "Look at all those **lovely** trees."

"Bet there are **WEREWOLVES** hiding

there," muttered Henry. "And I hope they come and eat you!"

"Mum!" squealed Peter. "Henry's trying to scare me."

"Don't be **horrid**, Henry," said Mum.

Horrid Henry looked around him. There was a gate, leading to endless meadows bordered by hedgerows. A **MUDDY** path wound through the trees and across the fields. A church spire stuck up in the distance.

"Right, I've seen the countryside, let's go home," said Henry.

Mum *glared* at him.

"What?" said Henry, scowling.

"Let's enjoy this *lovely* day," said Dad, sighing.

"So what do we do now?" said Henry.

"*Walk*," said Dad.

"Where?" said Henry.

"Just *walk*," said Mum, "and enjoy the *beautiful* scenery."

Henry groaned.

"We're heading for the lake," said

Dad, striding off. "I've brought bread and we can feed the ducks."

"But **Rapper Zapper** starts in an hour!"

"**TOUGH**," said Mum.

Mum, Dad and Peter headed through the gate into the field. Horrid Henry trailed behind them, walking as slowly as he could.

"Ahh, breathe the *lovely* fresh air," said Mum.

"We should do this more often," said Dad.

Henry sniffed.

The **HORRIBLE** smell of manure filled his nostrils.

"Ewww, smelly," said Henry. "Peter, couldn't you wait?"

"MUM!" shrieked Peter. "Henry called me smelly."

"Did not!"

"Did too!"

"Did not, smelly."

"WAAAAAAAAA!" wailed Peter. "Tell him to stop!"

"Don't be **horrid**, Henry!" screamed Mum. Her voice echoed. A dog walker passed her, and *glared*.

"Peter, would you rather run a mile, jump a stile, or eat a country *pancake*?" said Henry *sweetly*.

"Ooh," said Peter. "I love *pancakes*. And a country one must be even more delicious than a city one."

"**HA HA**," cackled Horrid Henry, sticking out his tongue. "Fooled you. Peter wants to eat **COWPATS!**"

"MUM!' screamed Peter.

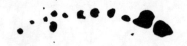

Henry walked.

And walked.

And walked.

His legs felt **HEAVIER**, and **HEAVIER**, and **HEAVIER**.

"This field is muddy," MOANED Henry.

"I'm bored," **groaned** Henry.

"My feet hurt," WHINED Henry.

"Can't we go home? We've already walked miles," WHINGED Henry.

"We've been walking for ten minutes," said Dad.

"Please can we go on walks more

often?" said Perfect Peter. "Oh, look at those *fluffy little sheepies!*"

Horrid Henry **pounced**. He was a **zombie** biting the head off the hapless human.

"AAAAEEEEEE!" squealed Peter.

"**Henry!**" screamed Mum.

"Stop it!" screamed Dad. "Or no TV for a week."

When he was king, thought Horrid Henry, any parent who made their children go on a hike would be **DUMPED** barefoot in a *scorpion-infested* desert.

Plod.
Plod.
Plod.

Horrid Henry *dragged* his feet.
Maybe his **horrible** MEAN parents
would get fed up waiting for him and
turn back, he thought, kicking some
mouldy leaves.

Squelch.
Squelch.
Squelch.

Oh no, not another MUDDY meadow.
And then suddenly Horrid Henry

had an idea. What was he thinking?
All that *fresh air* must be rotting
his brain. The sooner they got to the
stupid lake, the sooner they could get
home for the **Rapper Zapper** Zaps
Terminator Gladiator.

"Come on, everyone, let's run!"
shrieked Henry. "Race you down the
hill to the lake!"

"That's the spirit, Henry," said Dad.
Horrid Henry dashed past Dad.

"OW!" shrieked Dad,
tumbling into the
stinging nettles.

Horrid Henry **whizzed** past Mum.

"EWW!" shrieked Mum, slipping in a cowpat.

SPLAT!

Horrid Henry **pushed** past Peter.

"Waaa!" wailed Peter. "My wellies are getting dirty."

Horrid Henry scampered down the **MUDDY** path.

"Wait, Henry!" yelped Mum. "It's too slipp— **AAAiIIEEEEE!**"

Mum slid down the path on her bottom.

"Slow down!" puffed Dad.

"I can't run that fast," wailed Peter.

But **Horrid Henry** raced on.

"Shortcut across the field!" he called. "Come on, slowcoaches!" The black and white cow grazing alone in the

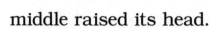

middle raised its head.

"**HENRY!**" shouted Dad.

Horrid Henry kept running.

"I don't think that's a cow!" shouted Mum.

The cow lowered its head and charged.

"**It's a bull!**" yelped Mum and Dad.

"**RUN!**"

"I said it was **dangerous** in the countryside!" gasped Henry, as everyone clambered over the stile in the nick of time. "Look, there's the lake!" he added, pointing.

Henry ran down to the water's edge. Peter followed. The embankment narrowed to a point. Peter *slipped* past Henry and bagged the best spot, right at the water's edge where the ducks gathered.

"Hey, get away from there," said Henry.

"I want to feed the ducks," said Peter.

"I want to feed the ducks,"
said Henry. "Now move."

"I was here first," said Peter.

"Not any more," said Henry.

Horrid Henry *pushed* Peter.

"Out of my way, **worm!**"

Perfect Peter pushed him back.

"Don't call me worm!"

Henry wobbled.

Peter wobbled.

Splash!

Peter tumbled into the lake.

Crash!

Henry tumbled into the lake.

"My babies!" shrieked Mum, jumping in after them.

"My – **glug glug glug**!" shrieked Dad, jumping into the muddy water after her.

"My new wellies!" gurgled Perfect Peter.

BANG!
Pow!
Terminator Gladiator slashed at
Rapper Zapper.
ZAP!
Rapper Zapper slashed back.
"**GO, Zappy!**" yelled Henry, lying
bundled up in blankets on the sofa.

Once everyone had scrambled out
of the lake, Mum and Dad had been
keen to get home as fast as possible.

"I think the park next time,"
mumbled Dad, sneezing.

"Definitely," mumbled Mum,
coughing.

"Oh, I don't know," said
Horrid Henry happily.
"A little water never
hurt anyone."

HORRID
HENRY
GOES SHOPPING

Horrid Henry stood in his bedroom up to his knees in clothes. The long-sleeve stripy T-shirt came to his elbow. His trousers stopped halfway down his legs. Henry sucked in his tummy as hard as he could. Still the zip wouldn't zip.

"Nothing fits!" he screamed, YANKING off the shirt and HURLING it across the room. "And my shoes hurt."

"All right, Henry, calm down," said Mum. "You've grown. We'll go out this afternoon and get you some new clothes and shoes."

"**NOOOOOO!**" shrieked Henry.
"**NOOOOOOOOOOO!**"

Horrid Henry **HATED** shopping.
Correction: Horrid Henry **LOVED**
shopping. He **LOVED** shopping for
gigantic TVs, *computer games*, COMICS,
toys and sweets. Yet for some reason
Horrid Henry's parents never wanted
to go shopping for good stuff. Oh
no. They shopped for Hoover bags.
Toothpaste. Spinach. Socks. Why oh
why did he have such **HORRIBLE**
parents? When he was grown-up

he'd never set foot in a supermarket. He'd only shop for TVs, *computer games* and *chocolate*.

But shopping for clothes was even worse than heaving his **HEAVY BONES** round the ⒽⒶⓅⓅⓎ ⓈⒽⓄⓅⓅⒺⓇ Supermarket. Nothing was more boring than being *dragged* round miles and miles and miles of shops,

filled with **disgusting** clothes only
a **MUTANT** would ever want to wear,
and then standing in a little room
while Mum made you try on **ICKY
SCRATCHY** things you wouldn't be seen
dead in if they were the last trousers
on earth. It was **horrible** enough
getting dressed once a day without
doing it fifty times. Just thinking
about trying on shirt after shirt after
shirt made Horrid Henry want to
scream.

"**I'M NOT GOING SHOPPING!**"
he howled, kicking the pile of clothes

as viciously as he could. "And you can't make me."

"What's all this yelling?" demanded Dad.

"Henry needs new trousers," said Mum grimly.

Dad went pale.

"Are you sure?"

"Yes," said Mum. "Take a look at him."

Dad looked at Henry. Henry SCOWLED.

"They're a little sᴍᴀʟʟ, but not that bad," said Dad.

"I can't **breathe** in these trousers!" shrieked Henry.

"That's why we're going shopping," said Mum. "And I'll take him." Last time Dad had taken Henry shopping for socks and came back instead with three Hairy Hellhound CDs and a jumbo pack of **Day-Glo slime**.

"I don't know what came over me," Dad had said, when Mum told him off.

"But why do I have to go?" said

Henry. "I don't want to waste my precious time shopping."

"What about my precious time?" said Mum.

Henry SCOWLED. Parents didn't have precious time. They were there to serve their children. New trousers should just magically appear, like clean clothes and packed lunches.

Mum's face brightened. "Wait, I have an idea," she *beamed*. She rushed out and came back with a large plastic bag. "Here," she said, pulling out a pair of BRIGHT RED

TROUSERS, "try these on."

Henry looked at them suspiciously.

"Where are they from?"

"Aunt Ruby dropped off some of Steve's old clothes a few weeks ago. I'm sure we'll find something that fits you."

Horrid Henry *stared* at Mum. Had she gone GAGA? Was she actually suggesting that he should wear his horrible cousin's mouldy old shirts and pongy pants? Just imagine, putting his arms into the same **STINKY** sleeves that Stuck-Up Steve had **slimed**? Uggh!

"**NO WAY!**" screamed Henry, shuddering. "I'm not wearing Steve's **smelly** old clothes. I'd catch rabies."

"They're practically brand new," said Mum.

"I don't care," said Henry.

"But Henry," said **Perfect Peter**, "I always wear your **HAND-ME-DOWNS**."

"So?" snarled Henry.

"I don't mind wearing **HAND-ME-DOWNS**,"

said Perfect Peter. "It saves so much money. You shouldn't be so **selfish**, Henry."

"Quite right, Peter," said Mum, smiling. "At least one of my sons thinks about others."

Horrid Henry *pounced*. He was a *vampire* sampling his supper.

"AAIIIEEEEEE!" squealed Peter.

"Stop that, Henry!" screamed Mum.

"Leave your brother alone!" screamed Dad.

Horrid Henry glared at Peter.

"Peter is a **worm**, Peter is a **toad**," jeered Henry.

"Mum!" wailed Peter. "Henry said I was a **worm**. And a **toad**."

"Don't be **HORRID**, Henry," said Dad. "Or no **TV** for a week. You have three choices. Wear Steve's old clothes. Wear your old clothes. Go shopping for new ones today."

"Do we have to go today?" moaned Henry.

"Fine," said Mum. "We'll go tomorrow."

"I don't want to go tomorrow," wailed Henry. "My weekend will be ruined."

Mum *glared* at Henry.

"Then we'll go right now this minute."

"**NO!**" screamed Horrid Henry.

"YES!" screamed Mum.

Several hours later, Mum and Henry walked into **MELLOW MALL**. Mum already looked like she'd been crossing the **Sahara desert** without water for days. Serve her right for bringing

me here, thought **Horrid Henry**, scowling, as he scuffed his feet. "Can't we go to SHOP 'N' DROP?" whined Henry. "Graham says they've got a win-your-weight-in-chocolate competition."

"No," said Mum, *dragging* Henry into *Zippy's Department Store*. "We're here

to get you some new trousers and shoes. Now hurry up, we don't have all day."

Horrid Henry looked around. **WOW!** There was lots of great stuff on display.

"I want the **Hip-Hop Robots**," said Henry.

"No," said Mum.

"I want the new **Supersoaker!**" screeched Henry.

"No," said Mum.

"I want a **Creepy Crawly** lunchbox!"

"**NO!**" said Mum, pulling him into

the boys' clothing department.

What, thought **Horrid Henry** grimly, is the point of going shopping if you never buy anything?

"I want **ROOT-A-TOOT** trainers with flashing red lights," said Henry. He

could see himself
now, strolling
into class, a
bugle blasting

and red light flashing every time his
feet hit the floor. COOL! He'd love to
see Miss Battle-Axe's face when he
exploded into class wearing them.

"No," said Mum, shuddering.

"Oh please," said Henry.

"NO!" said Mum. "We're here to buy
trousers and sensible school shoes."

"But I want ROOT-A-TOOT trainers!"
screamed Horrid Henry. "Why can't

we buy what I want to buy? You're the **MEANEST** mother in the world and I hate you!"

"Don't be **horrid**, Henry. Go and try these on," said Mum, *grabbing* a selection of **hideous** trousers and **revolting** T-shirts. "I'll keep looking."

Horrid Henry sighed loudly and slumped towards the dressing room. No one in the world suffered as much as he did. Maybe he could hide between the clothes racks and never come out.

Then something **WONDERFUL** in

the toy department next door caught his eye.

whooa! A whole row of the new *megalotronic animobotic robots* with 213 programmable actions. Horrid Henry dumped the clothes and ran over to have a look. Oooh, the new Intergalactic Samurai Gorillas which launched real *stinkbombs!* And the latest **Supersoakers!**

And deluxe **Dungeon Drink** kits with a celebrity chef recipe book! To say nothing of the **MEGA·WHIRL GOO SHOOTER** which sprayed **fluorescent goo** for fifty metres in every direction. **WOW!**

Mum staggered into the dressing room with more clothes. "Henry?" said Mum.

No reply.

"HENRY!" said Mum.

Still no reply.

Mum *yanked* open a dressing room door.

"Hen—"

"EXCUSE ME!" yelped a bald man, standing in his underpants.

"Sorry," said Mum, blushing bright pink. She dashed out of the changing room and scanned the shop floor.

Henry was gone.

Mum searched *up* the aisles.

No Henry.

Mum searched *down* the aisles.

Still no Henry.

Then Mum saw a tuft of hair sticking up behind the neon sign for **BALLISTIC BAZOOKA BOOMERANGS**. She marched over and hauled Henry away.

"I was just looking," protested Henry.

Henry tried on one pair of trousers after another.

"**NO, NO, NO, NO, NO, NO, NO**," said Henry, kicking off the final pair. "I hate all of them."

"All right," said Mum, grimly. "We'll look somewhere else."

Mum and Henry went to **TOP TROUSERS**. They went to ***Cool Clothes***. They went to **Stomp in the Swamp**. Nothing had been right.

"Too tight," moaned Henry.

"TOO ITCHY!"

"Too big!"

"Too small!"

"Too ugly!"

"Too red!"

"**TOO UNCOMFORTABLE!**"

"We're going to *Tip-Top Togs*," said Mum wearily. "The first thing that fits, we're buying."

Mum staggered into the children's department and grabbed a pair of

pink and green tartan trousers in Henry's size.

"Try these on," she ordered. "If they fit we're having them."

Horrid Henry *gazed* in horror at the horrendous trousers.

"Those are *girls'* trousers!" he screamed.

"They are not," said Mum.

"**ARE TOO!**" shrieked Henry.

"I'm sick and tired of your excuses, Henry," said Mum. "Put them on or no pocket money for a year. I mean it."

Horrid Henry put on the **pink and green tartan trousers**, puffing out his stomach as much as possible. Not even Mum would make him buy trousers that were TOO TIGHT.

Oh no. The **HORRIBLE** trousers had an elastic waist. They would fit a mouse as easily as an **ELEPHANT**.

"And lots of room to grow," said Mum brightly. "You can wear them for years. Perfect."

"**NOOOOOO!**" howled Henry. He flung himself on the floor kicking and screaming.

"NOOOO! THEY'RE GIRLS' TROUSERS!!!"

"We're buying them," said Mum. She gathered up the **tartan trousers** and stomped over to the till. She tried not to think about starting all over again trying to find a pair of shoes that Henry would wear.

A little girl in pigtails walked out of the dressing room, twirling in

**pink and green
tartan trousers**.

"I love them,
Mummy!" she
shrieked. "Let's
get three pairs."

Horrid Henry stopped howling.

He looked at Mum.

Mum looked at Henry.

Then they both looked at the
pink and green tartan trousers
Mum was carrying.

ROOT-A-TOOT!
ROOT-A-TOOT!
ROOT-A-TOOT!
TOOT! TOOT!

An earsplitting bugle blast shook
the house. Flashing red lights
bounced off the walls.

"What's that noise?"
said Dad, covering
his ears.

"What noise?" said
Mum, pretending
to read.

ROOT-A-TOOT!
ROOT-A-TOOT!
ROOT-A-TOOT!
TOOT! TOOT!

Dad *stared* at Mum.

"You didn't," said Dad. "Not –

ROOT-A-TOOT trainers?"

Mum hid her face in her hands.

"I don't know what came over me," said Mum.

HORRID HENRY'S
CAR JOURNEY

"Henry! We're waiting!"
"Henry! Get down here!"
"Henry! I'm warning you!"
Horrid Henry sat on his bed and SCOWLED. His MEAN, horrible parents could warn him all they liked. He wasn't moving.

"HENRY! We're going to be late," yelled Mum.

"Good!" shouted Henry.

"HENRY! This is your final warning," yelled Dad.

"I DON'T WANT TO GO TO POLLY'S!" screamed Henry.

"I want to go to Ralph's birthday party."

Mum **stomped** upstairs.

"Well you can't," said Mum. "You're coming to the christening, and that's that."

"**NO!**" screeched Henry. "I **HATE** Polly, I **HATE** babies, and I **HATE** you!"

Henry had been a page boy at the wedding of his cousin, *Prissy Polly*, when she'd married PIMPLY PAUL. Now they had a *prissy*, PIMPLY baby, Vomiting Vera.

Henry had met Vera once before.

She'd
thrown up
all over him. Henry had hoped never
to see her again until she was grown
up and behind bars, but no such
luck. He had to go and watch her
be **dunked** in a vat of water, on the
same day that Ralph was having
a birthday party at **Goo-Shooter
World**. Henry had been longing for
ages to go to **Goo-Shooter World**.
Today was his chance. His only
chance. But no. Everything was
RUINED.

Perfect Peter poked his head round the door.

"*I'm* all ready, Mum," said Perfect Peter. His shoes were polished, his teeth were **brushed**, and his hair neatly **COMBED**. "I know how annoying it is to be kept waiting when you're in a rush."

"Thank you, darling Peter," said Mum. "At least one of my children knows how to behave."

Horrid Henry **ROARED** and **ATTACKED**. He was a *swooping* vulture digging his

claws into a dead MOUSE.

"AAAAAAAAAEEEEE!" squealed Peter.

"Stop being **horrid**, Henry!" said Mum.

"No one told me it was today!" screeched Henry.

"Yes we did," said Mum. "But you weren't paying attention."

"As usual," said Dad.

"*I knew we were going*," said Peter.

"**I DON'T WANT TO GO TO POLLY'S!**"

screamed Henry. "I want to go to Ralph's!"

"Get in the car — **NOW**!" said Dad.

"Or no TV for a year!" said Mum.

EEEK! Horrid Henry stopped wailing. No TV for a year. Anything was better than that.

Grimly, he **stomped** down the stairs and out the front door. They wanted him in the car. They'd have him in the car.

"Don't **SLAM** the door," said Mum.

SLAM!

Horrid Henry *pushed* Peter away from
the car door and scrambled for the
right-hand side behind the driver.
Perfect Peter **GRABBED** his legs and
tried to climb over him.

VICTORY! Henry got
there first.

Henry liked sitting on the right-

hand side so he could watch the
speedometer.

Peter liked sitting on the right-
hand side so he could watch the
speedometer.

"Mum," said Peter. "It's my turn to
sit on the right!"

"No it isn't," said Henry. "It's mine."

"MINE!"

"MINE!"

"We haven't even left and already
you're fighting?" said Dad.

"You'll take turns," said Mum. "You
can swap after we stop."

Vroom. Vroom.

Dad started the car.

The doors locked.

Horrid Henry was trapped.

But wait. Was there a glimmer of hope? Was there a TEENY TINY chance? What was it Mum always said when he and Peter were *squabbling* in the car? "If you don't stop fighting I'm going to turn around and go home!" And wasn't home just exactly where he wanted to be? All he had to do was to do what he did best.

"Could I have a story CD please?"

said Perfect Peter.

"No! I want a **music CD**," said Horrid Henry.

"I want 'Mouse Goes to Town'," said Peter.

"I want '**Driller Cannibals' Greatest Hits**'," said Henry.

"Story!"

"**Music!**"

"Story!"

"**Music!**"

SMACK!
SMACK!

"Waaaaaa!"

"Stop it, Henry," said Mum.

"Tell Peter to leave me alone!"
screamed Henry.

"Tell Henry to leave me alone!"
screamed Peter.

"Leave each other alone," said Mum.

Horrid Henry *glared* at Perfect Peter.

Perfect Peter *glared* at Horrid Henry.

Horrid Henry **stretched**. Slowly,
steadily, centimetre by centimetre, he
spread out into Peter's area.

"Henry's on my side!"

"No I'm not!"

"Henry, leave Peter alone," said Dad.
"I mean it."

"I'm not doing anything," said
Henry. "ARE WE THERE YET?"

"No," said Dad.

Thirty seconds passed.

"ARE WE THERE YET?" said Horrid Henry.

"No!" said Mum.

"ARE WE THERE YET?" said Horrid Henry.

"NO!" screamed Mum and Dad.

"We only left ten minutes ago,"
said Dad.

Ten minutes! Horrid Henry felt as if
they'd been travelling for hours.

"Are we a quarter of the way there
yet?"

"NO!"

"Are we halfway there yet?"

"NO!!"

"How much longer until we're halfway there?"

"**STOP IT, HENRY!**" screamed Mum.

"You're driving me **CRAZY!**" screamed Dad. "Now be quiet and leave us alone."

Henry sighed. Boy, was this boring. Why didn't they have a decent car, with **BUILT-IN VIDEO GAMES, MOVIES**, and **jacuzzi?** That's just what he'd have, when he was king.

Softly, he started to **HUM** under his breath.

"Henry's HUMMING!"

"Stop being **horrid**, Henry!"

"I'm not doing anything," protested Henry. He lifted his foot.

"MUM!" squealed Peter. "Henry's **kicking** me."

"Are you **kicking** him, Henry?"

"Not yet," muttered Henry. Then he screamed.

"MUM! PETER'S LOOKING OUT OF MY WINDOW!"

"Dad! Henry's looking out of *my* window."

"Peter *breathed* on me."

"Henry's *breathing* loud on purpose."

"Henry's **STARING** at me."

"Peter's on my side!"

"TELL HIM TO STOP!"
screamed Henry and Peter.

Mum's face was **RED**.

Dad's face was **RED**.

"THAT'S IT!" screamed Dad.

"I can't take this any more!"
screamed Mum.

Yes! thought Henry. We're going
to turn back!

But instead of turning round,
the car *screeched* to a halt at the

motorway services.

"We're going to take a break," said
Mum. She looked exhausted.

"Who needs a **wee**?" said Dad.
He looked even worse.

"Me," said Peter.

"Henry?"

"No," said Henry. He wasn't a baby. He
knew when he needed a **wee** and he

didn't need one now.

"This is our only stop, Henry," said Mum. "I think you should go."

"**NO!**" screamed Henry. Several people looked up. "I'll wait in the car."

Mum and Dad were too tired to argue. They disappeared into the services with Peter.

RATS. Despite his best efforts, it looked like Mum and Dad were going to carry on. Well, if he couldn't make them turn back, maybe he could *delay* them? Somehow? Suddenly Henry had a *wonderful,*

SPECTACULAR idea. It couldn't be easier, and it was guaranteed to work. He'd miss the christening!

Mum, Dad, and Peter got back in the car. Mum drove off.

"I need a **wee**," said Henry.

"Not now, Henry."

"I NEED A WEE!" screamed Henry. **"NOW!"**

Mum headed back to the services.

Dad and Henry went to the toilets.

"I'll wait for you outside," said Dad. "Hurry up or we'll be late."

Late! What a *lovely* word.

Henry went into the toilet and locked the door. Then he **waited**. And **waited**. And **waited**.

Finally, he heard Dad's grumpy voice.

"Henry? Have you fallen in?"

Henry rattled the door.

"I'm locked in," said Henry. "The door's **STUCK**. I can't get out."

"Try, Henry," pleaded Dad.

"I have," said Henry. "I guess they'll have to break the door down."

That should take a few hours. He settled himself on the toilet seat and got out a **COMIC**.

"Or you could just *crawl* underneath the partition into the next stall," said Dad.

AAARGGHH. Henry could have **burst** into tears. Wasn't it just his rotten luck to try to get locked in a toilet which had gaps on the sides? Henry didn't much fancy *wriggling* round on the cold floor. Sighing, he gave the stall door a tug and opened it.

Horrid Henry sat in silence for the rest of the trip. He was so DEPRESSED he didn't even protest when Peter demanded his turn on the right. Plus, he felt **car sick**.

Henry rolled down his window.

"Mum!" said Peter. "I'm cold."

Dad turned the heat on.

"Having the heat on makes me feel **sick**," said Henry.

"I'm going to be **sick!**" whimpered Peter.

"I'm going to be **sick**," whined Henry.

"But we're almost there," screeched Mum. "Can't you hold on until—"

BLECCCHH.

Peter threw up all over Mum.

BLECCCHH.

Henry threw up all over Dad.

The car pulled into the driveway.

Mum and Dad s t a g g e r e d out of the car to Polly's front door.

"We survived," said Mum, mopping her dress.

"Thank God that's over," said Dad,

mopping his shirt.

Horrid Henry SCUFFED his feet
sadly behind them. Despite all his
hard work, he'd lost the battle. While
Rude Ralph and Dizzy
Dave and Jolly Josh
were *dashing* about
spraying each other
with **green goo**
later this afternoon
he'd be stuck at a
boring party with lots
of grown-ups YAK YAK YAKKING.
Oh misery!

DING DONG.

The door opened.

It was *Prissy Polly*.

She was in her bathrobe and slippers. She carried a **STINKY**, smelly, wailing baby over her shoulder. PIMPLY PAUL followed. He was wearing a **FILTHY** T-shirt with **sick** down the front.

"EEEEK," squeaked Polly.

Mum tried to look as if she had not

been through **HELL** and barely lived
to tell the tale.

"We're here!" said Mum brightly.
"How's the lovely baby?"

"Too *prissy*," said Polly.

"Too PIMPLY," said Paul.

Polly and Paul looked at Mum and
Dad.

"What are you doing here?" said
Polly finally.

"We're here for the christening,"
said Mum.

"Vera's christening?" said Polly.

"It's *next* weekend," said Paul.

Mum looked like she wanted to sag to the floor.

Dad looked like he wanted to sag beside her.

"We've come on the wrong day?" whispered Mum.

"You mean, we have to go and come back?" whispered Dad.

"Yes," said Polly.

"Oh no," said Mum.

"Oh no," said Dad.

"**BLECCCHH**," vomited Vera.

"EEEEK!" wailed Polly. "Gotta go."

She **slammed** the door.

"You mean, we can go home?" said Henry. "Now?"

"Yes," whispered Mum.

"whoopee!" screamed Henry. "Hang on, Ralph, here I come!"

HORRID HENRY'S

HOBBY

"Out of my way, worm!" shrieked Horrid Henry, pushing past his younger brother Perfect Peter and dashing into the kitchen.

"NO!" screamed Perfect Peter. He scrambled after Henry and clutched his leg.

"Get off me!" shouted Henry. He grabbed the unopened SWEET TWEET cereal box. "**Nah nah ne nah nah**, I got it first."

Perfect Peter lunged for the Sweet Tweet box and snatched it from Henry. "But it's my turn!"

"NO, MINE!" shrieked Henry.

He ripped open the top and stuck his hand inside.

"It's mine!" shrieked Peter. He ripped open the bottom.

A small wrapped toy fell to the floor.

Henry and Peter both *lunged* for it.

"GIMME THAT!" yelled Henry.

"But it's my turn to have it!" yelled Peter.

"Stop being **horrid**, Henry!" shouted Mum. "Now give me that thing!"

Henry and Peter both held on tight.

168

"NO!" screamed Henry and Peter. **"IT'S MY TURN TO HAVE THE TOY!"**

Horrid Henry and Perfect Peter both collected **GIZMOS** from inside **SWEET TWEET** cereal boxes. So did everyone at their school. There were ten different coloured **GIZMOS** to collect, from the common green to the rare gold. Both Henry and

Peter had **GIZMOS** of every colour. Except for one. Gold.

"Right," said Mum, "whose turn is it to get the toy?"

"**MINE!**" screamed Henry and Peter.

"He got the last one!" screeched Henry. "Remember — he opened the new box and got the blue **GIZMO**."

It was true that Perfect Peter had got the blue **GIZMO** — two boxes ago.

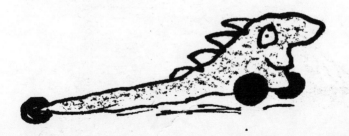

But why should Peter get any? If he hadn't started collecting GIZMOS to copy me, thought Henry resentfully, I'd get every single one.

"NO!" howled Peter. He burst into tears. "Henry opened the last box."

"Cry-baby," jeered Henry.

"**STOP IT**," said Peter.

"**Stop it**," mimicked Henry.

"Mum, Henry's teasing me," wailed Peter.

"I remember now," said Mum. "It's Peter's turn."

"Thank you, Mum," said Perfect Peter.

"IT'S NOT FAIR!" screamed Horrid Henry as Peter tore open the wrapping. There was a *gold* gleam.

"Oh my goodness," gasped Peter. **"A GOLD GIZMO!"**

Horrid Henry felt as if he'd been punched in the stomach. He stared at the glorious, *glowing*, golden GIZMO.

"It's not fair!" howled Henry. "I want a gold GIZMO!"

"I'm sorry, Henry," said Mum. "It'll be your turn next."

"But I want the gold one!" SCREAMED Henry.

He leapt on Peter and yanked the GIZMO out of his hand.

He was *Hurricane Henry* uprooting everything in his path.

"HELLLLLLLLP!" howled Peter.

"Stop being **horrid**, Henry, or no more Gizmos for you!" shouted Mum. "Now clean up this **mess** and get dressed."

"NO!" howled Henry. He ran upstairs to his room, slamming the door behind him.

He had to have a gold GIZMO. He simply had to. No one at school had a gold one. Henry could see himself now, the centre of attention, everyone

174

pushing and **SHOVING** just to get a look at his gold GIZMO. Henry could charge 20p a peek. **Everyone** would want to see it and to hold it. Henry would be invited to every birthday party. Instead, Peter would be the star attraction. Henry GNASHED his teeth just thinking about it.

But how could he get one? You couldn't buy GIZMOS. You could only get them inside SWEET TWEET cereal boxes. Mum was so mean she made Henry and Peter finish the old box before she'd buy a new

one. Henry had eaten **MOUNTAINS** of **SWEET TWEET** cereal to collect all his 𝒢𝐼ℤ𝑀𝒪𝒮. All that hard work would be in vain, unless he got a *gold* one.

He could, of course, *steal* Peter's. But Peter would be sure to notice, and Henry would be the chief suspect.

He could **swap**. Yes! He would offer Peter *two* greens! That was generous. In fact, that was really generous. But Peter hated doing swaps. For some reason he always thought Henry was trying to cheat him.

And then suddenly Henry had a
brilliant, SPECTACULAR idea.
True, it did involve a little TINY TEENSY WEENSY
bit of trickery, but Henry's cause was
just. *He'd* been collecting GIZMOS far
longer than Peter had. He deserved
a gold one, and Peter didn't.

"So, you got a gold GIZMO," said
Henry, popping into Peter's room.
"I'm really sorry."

Perfect Peter looked up from
polishing his GIZMOS. "Why?" he
said suspiciously. "EVERYONE wants
a gold GIZMO."

177

Horrid Henry looked sadly at Perfect Peter. "Not any more. They're very unlucky, you know. Every single person who's got one has died **horribly**."

Perfect Peter stared at Henry, then at his golden GIZMO.

"That's not true, Henry."

"Yes it is."

"No it isn't."

Horrid Henry walked slowly around Peter's room. Every so often he made a LITTLE note in a notebook.

"Marbles, check. Three knights,

check. Nature kit — nah. Coin collection, check."

"What are you doing?" said Peter.

"Just looking round your stuff to see what I want when you're gone."

STOP IT!" said Peter. "You just made that up about gold GIZMOS — didn't you?"

"No," said Henry. "It's in all the newspapers. There was the boy out walking his dog who fell into a pit of **molten lava**. There was the girl who

drowned in the **loo**, and then that poor boy who—"

"I don't want to **DIE**," said Perfect Peter. He looked pale. "What am I going to do?"

Henry paused. "There's nothing you can do. Once you've got it you're **Sunk**."

Peter jumped up.

"I'll throw it away!"

"That wouldn't work," said Henry. "You'd still be *jinxed*. There's only one way out—"

"What?" said Perfect Peter.

"If you give the gold away to someone **BRAVE** enough to take it, then the jinx passes to them."

"But no one will take it from me!" WAILED Peter.

"Tell you what," said Henry. "I'll take the risk."

"Are you sure?" said Peter.

"Of course," said **Horrid Henry**. "You're my brother. You'd risk your life for me."

"Okay," said Peter. He handed Henry the gold **GIZMO**. "Thank you, Henry.

You're the best brother in the world."

"I know," said Horrid Henry.

He actually had his very own gold GIZMO in his hand. It was his, fair and square. He couldn't wait to see MOODY MARGARET'S face when he waved it in front of her. And Rude Ralph. He would be green with envy.

Then Perfect Peter BURST into tears and ran downstairs.

"Mum!" he wailed. "Henry's going to die! And it's all my fault."

"WHAT?" screeched Mum.
Uh oh, thought Henry. He clutched

his treasure.

Mum **STORMED** upstairs. She snatched the *gold* **GIZMO** from Henry.

"How could you be so **horrid,** Henry?" shouted Mum. "No TV for a week! Poor Peter. Now get ready. We're going shopping."

"**NO!**" howled Henry. "**I'M NOT GOING!**"

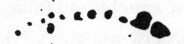

Horrid Henry scowled as he followed Mum up and down the aisles of the **HAPPY SHOPPER**.

He'd **crashed** the cart into some
people so Mum wouldn't let him push
it. Then she caught him filling the
cart with **CRISPS** and FIZZY drinks
and made him put them all back.
What a **horrible ROTTEN** day
this had turned out to be.

"Yum, cabbage," said Perfect Peter.
"Could we get some?"

"Certainly," said Mum.

"And beetroot, my
favourite!" said Peter.

"Help yourself," said Mum.

"I want sweets!" screamed Henry.

"No," said Mum.

"I WANT DOUGHNUTS!" screamed
Henry.

"**No!**" screamed Mum.

"There's nothing to eat here!"
shrieked Henry.

"Stop being **horrid**, Henry," hissed

Mum. "Everyone's looking."

"I don't care."

"Well I do," said Mum. "Now make yourself useful. Go and get a box of **SWEET TWEETS**."

"All right," said Henry. Now was his chance to escape. Before Mum could stop him he **grabbed** a cart and *whizzed* off.

"Watch out for the racing driver!" squealed Henry. Shoppers **scattered** as he *zoomed* down the aisle and **screeched** to a halt in front of the cereal section. There were the **SWEET TWEETS**. A huge pile of them, in a display tower, under a twinkling sign saying, "A free **GIZMO** in every box! Collect them all!"

Henry reached for a box and put it in his cart.

And then **Horrid Henry** stopped. What was the point of buying a whole box if it just contained another

green GIZMO? Henry didn't think he could bear it. I'll just check what's inside, he thought. Then, if it *is* a green one, I'll be prepared for the disappointment.

Carefully, he opened the box and slipped his hand inside. **AHA!** There was the toy. He lifted it out, and held it up to the light. **RATS!** A green GIZMO, just what he'd feared.

But wait. There was bound to be a child out there longing for a green GIZMO to complete his collection just as much as Henry was longing for a gold. Wouldn't it be selfish and **horrid** of Henry to take a green he didn't need when it would make someone else so happy?

I'll just PEEK inside one more box, thought Horrid Henry, replacing the box he'd opened and reaching for another.

Rip! He tore it open. Red.

Hmmm, thought Henry. Red is surplus to requirements.

Rip! Another box opened. Blue.

Rip! Rip! Rip!

Green! Green! Blue!

I'll just try one more at the back,
thought Henry. He stood on tiptoe,
and **stretched** as far as he could.
His hand reached inside the box and
grabbed hold of the toy.

The tower **WOBBLED**.

CRASH!

Horrid Henry sprawled on the ground. Henry was covered in **SWEET TWEETS**. So was the floor. So were all the shoppers.

"**HELP!**" screamed the manager, skidding in the mess. "Whose **horrid** boy is this?"

There was a very long silence.

"Mine," WHISPERED Mum.

Horrid Henry sat in the kitchen surrounded by **BOXES** and **BOXES** and **BOXES** of **SWEET TWEETS**. He'd be eating **SWEET TWEETS** for breakfast, lunch and dinner for weeks. But it was worth it, thought Henry happily. Banned for life from the Happy Shopper, how wonderful. He uncurled his hand to enjoy again the glint of *gold*.

Although he had noticed that **SCRUMMY YUMMIES** were offering a free Twizzle card in every box. Hmmm, Twizzle cards.

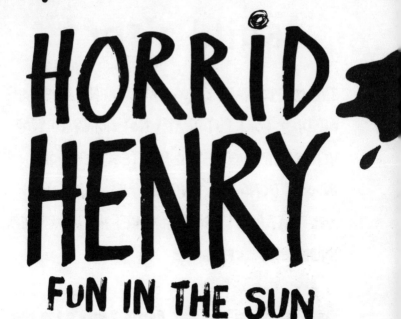

HORRID HENRY

FUN IN THE SUN

Turn the page for
lots of fun games
and activities!

Build a Fort

THE PURPLE HAND GANG HAVE BEEN RAINED OUT OF THEIR FORT BUT THAT'S NOT GOING TO STOP HENRY! HE'S DECIDED TO CREATE A NEW FORT INDOORS USING THE DINING CHAIRS, THE SOFA AND THAT REALLY POSH BLANKET HIS MUM KEEPS HIDDEN IN A CUPBOARD.

Build your own fort with Horrid Henry's top tips:

1. A great fort needs great **SNACKS**. Stock your fort with crisps, chocolate and biscuits — absolutely no vegetables allowed.

2. A fort has to be comfy so make sure you fill it with pillows and blankets so that you can sit and do nothing all day.

3. Positioning is crucial. You should always be able to see the TV or how would you watch it?

4. A fort is the perfect place to keep toys and **COMIC** books. You'll never be bored.

5. It can get dark in a fort so bring a torch. Bonus: shine the light in people's faces when they try to come in.

6. You need a strong password: a fort is your castle. No password, no entry.

7. Make a **KEEP OUT** sign. Perfect Peter never gets the message without one.

8. Remember spare **pillows** to throw at intruders.

9. Build your fort against a wall or two, so there is less to defend from attackers.

10. Find some hiding spots for stowing your best **SNACKS** – just in case!

Identify the character

THINK YOU KNOW CLEVER CLARE FROM SOUR SUSAN? TEST YOUR SKILLS BELOW AND SEE IF YOU CAN MATCH THE CHARACTER TO THEIR SHADOW:

- **Horrid Henry**
- **Perfect Peter**
- **Moody Margaret**
- **Mum**
- **Rude Ralph**
- **Miss Battle-Axe**

Turn to the back of the book for the answers.

Treasure Hunt

PERFECT PETER KEEPS SAYING HE'S BORED – HE'S ALREADY DONE ALL OF HIS HOLIDAY HOMEWORK! HENRY DECIDES TO ENTERTAIN HIM WITH A TREASURE HUNT. HENRY HAS HIDDEN ALL OF THE STAMPS IN PETER'S COLLECTION FOR PETER TO FIND.

Organise your own treasure hunt with these tips:

1. Decide what you're going to hide. TOYS and sweets work well.

2. Hide your treasure. Make sure you write down where you've hidden it just in case.

3. Draw a map and mark a big **X** where your treasure is.

4. Give your map to your friend to see if they can find the treasure.

5. For extra fun, both of you can hide treasure and make a map, then race to see who can find the other's treasure first.

invisible Ink

HORRID HENRY KEEPS INTERCEPTING THE SECRET
CLUB'S MESSAGES! LUCKILY MOODY MARGARET HAS
DISCOVERED THE PERFECT WAY TO KEEP MESSAGES
FROM HIM – INVISIBLE INK. LEARN HOW TO MAKE
YOUR OWN:

You will need:

Lemon juice

Paper

Lamp or other light bulb

A paint brush or cotton bud

Instructions:

1. Squeeze some lemon juice into a bowl and add a few drops of water.

2. Mix the water and lemon juice with a spoon.

3. Use your paint brush or cotton bud to

write a message on paper with the
mixture.

4. Wait for the juice to dry so it becomes
   completely invisible.

5. To read the message, hold it up to a
   lightbulb until it gets warm.

Rock Star!

HENRY HAS DECIDED TO BECOME FAMOUS, JUST LIKE HIS FAVOURITE BAND THE KILLER BOY RATS. ALL HE NEEDS TO DO IS FORM A BAND AND THROW A CONCERT. AND FOR THAT HE NEEDS HIS FRIENDS AND SOME MUSICAL INSTRUMENTS. FORM YOUR OWN BAND BY MAKING SOME INSTRUMENTS:

A RAINSTICK

You will need:

A water bottle

Rice or beads

Instructions:

1. Half-fill an empty water bottle with rice or beads.

2. Decorate your rainstick so that it rocks.

3. Slowly tilt the bottle upside down to make the sound of rain.

A HARMONICA

You will need:

Drinking straws

Scissors

Tape

Instructions:

1. Get 12-16 straws and cut them in pairs to different lengths so that you have two of each length.

2. Get a long strip of sticky tape and put the straws on the sticky side, arranging them in twos from the shortest to the longest ones.

3. Wrap tape around your harmonica.

4. Blow into the straws to create music.

DRUMS

You will need:

A tin can

A balloon

An elastic band

Anything stick-like for your drumstick — a
pencil works well!

Instructions:

1. Make sure you have an adult's help when
   working with the tin can. It should have
   its lid removed and be clean.

2. Cut the tip of the balloon off and stretch it over the can.
3. Secure the balloon with an elastic band
4. Hit the balloon with your drumstick to make noise.

NO SPARE TIN CANS? TRY BASHING A STICK ON A TUBE OF CRISPS, A YOGHURT POT OR A STORAGE TUB.

GUITAR
You will need:

A small box
Elastic bands

Instructions:

1. Take the lid off the box.
2. With an adult's help, stretch the elastic bands over the open box.
3. Strum the elastic to make sounds.

Would You Rather?

HENRY'S MOTHER HAS ASKED HIM IF HE WANTS PEAS OR CARROTS WITH DINNER. NEITHER!

Here are some of Henry's other favourite impossible choices to offer his friends.

1. Would you rather pick Miss Lovely's nose or smell Miss Battle-Axe's feet?
2. Would you rather have a robot or a rocket?
3. Would you rather have super strength or be able to fly?

4. Would you rather get all of Stuck-Up Steve's presents for a year and then only get stamps for Perfect Peter's stamp collection for three years, or never get any presents and then get whatever you want for a day?

5. Would you rather get to eat whatever you wanted or go to bed whenever you wanted?

6. Would you rather turn up to school in your underwear or wet yourself during class?

7. Would you rather have hands for feet or feet for hands?

8. Would you rather have everyone believe every lie you ever told or be able to tell when people lie to you?

9. Would you rather not be allowed to eat any sweets for a year or not be allowed to watch TV for a year?

10. Would you rather share a bedroom with Perfect Peter or have to spend an hour with the Bogey Babysitter every day?

wordsearch

HORRID HENRY IS GOING ON HOLIDAY! CAN YOU
FIND ALL THE ITEMS HE IS TRYING TO FIT
INTO HIS SUITCASE?

K	T	E	D	D	Y	K	F	F	H	Q	S
R	E	K	A	O	S	R	E	P	U	S	E
C	P	T	F	C	O	M	I	C	S	G	B
R	R	B	G	H	F	C	U	O	U	H	U
I	Y	O	Q	L	O	K	U	W	Q	S	Q
S	C	H	O	C	O	L	A	T	E	W	H
P	X	D	U	F	T	N	D	P	Q	E	K
S	Z	B	L	J	B	S	F	R	J	E	L
V	G	R	V	W	A	K	I	F	L	T	C
U	U	A	P	T	L	U	O	I	S	S	E
D	V	O	W	D	I	E	E	M	M	L	S
N	O	I	S	I	V	E	L	E	T	E	Y

Television   Comics   Slime
Crisps   Sweets   Teddy
Chocolate   Super Soaker   Football

Turn to the back of the book for the answers.

Super Spy

THE PURPLE HAND GANG IS UP
TO SOMETHING! THEY HAVE
BEEN GATHERING EVERY
DAY FOR THE LAST WEEK.
IT'S TIME THE SECRET CLUB
FOUND OUT WHAT THEY'RE
PLANNING.

Moody Margaret's guide to becoming a super sleuth:

1. Get a notebook and write down
   EVERYTHING you observe. No detail is
   too small! Fill in a few pages first with
   homework or recipes so no one suspects
   you of spy work.

2. Be selective in your recruits. You'll get
   more done with friends but be wary of a
   big group. It's hard to be secret with so

many of you!

3. Use a code! Margaret likes to write in numbers, where each number has a different letter assigned.

4. Make sure your base of operations is secure! Scout it out for intruders before saying anything secret.

5. Hide **EVERYTHING** and leave decoy replacements. No one will keep looking for your secret spy diary if they find a fake one first!

6. Know your enemy! When do they eat, when do they sleep, what's their *favourite* snack and what's their favourite toy?

7. Blend in with your surroundings. Use camouflage and disguise whenever you can.

8. Use code names. That way no one will know what you're talking about if you're overheard.

Make a Kite

STUCK-UP STEVE JUST GOT THE NEW MONSTER MASHER KITE AND HENRY'S PARENTS ARE REFUSING TO BUY HIM ONE! HE'S GOING TO MAKE HIS OWN AND IT'S GOING TO BE EVEN COOLER THAN THE MONSTER MASHER. HIS KITE WILL HAVE THE JOLLY ROGER, RACING STRIPES, CAMOUFLAGE AND A HUGE DRAWING OF STEVE'S KITE ON FIRE!

Make your own kite with these instructions.
You will need:

Sticks

Paper

String

Tape

Instructions:

1. Decorate your piece of paper.

2. Tape your two sticks together to form a cross.

3. Tape the cross on to the back of the paper.

4. Tie some string on to the cross and make sure you have enough to let your kite fly high!

comic Book

HORRID HENRY LOVES COMIC BOOKS BUT HE'S
DECIDED HE CAN MAKE A MUCH BETTER COMIC
THAN ANY OF THE ADULTS WHO WRITE THEM.

CREATE YOUR OWN COMIC BOOK BELOW:

Road Trip

HENRY IS BEING TAKEN ON HIS LEAST FAVOURITE SUMMER ACTIVITY: VISITING PRISSY POLLY, PIMPLY PAUL AND VOMITING VERA! YUK! THEY LIVE SO FAR AWAY AND THERE'S NO TV IN THE CAR. LUCKILY, HENRY CAN ALWAYS PLAY BACKSEAT BINGO TO PASS THE TIME!

ARE YOU IN THE CAR ON A LONG JOURNEY? KEEP YOUR EYE OUT FOR SOME OF HENRY'S FAVOURITE THINGS TO SEE. IF YOU GET THE WHOLE LIST, YELL **"BINGO!"**

• A person singing along to the radio (even better if they're dancing too!)

- A dog in the back seat (bonus point if there's more than one)
- A plane (probably full of people going somewhere way more interesting!)
- Animals in a field (they're not being forced to go on a boring visit!)
- A yellow car (bonus point if it's a convertible)
- Someone riding their bike (half a point for a motorbike)
- Roadworks (great, now it's going to take even longer!)
- Birds (look how free they are!)
- A police car (bonus point if the siren is on)
- A stop sign (maybe now you can convince your parents to turn round)
- A train (a much more fun way to travel)
- A tractor (bonus point if you're not stuck behind it)

Sports Day

HENRY'S WON HIS FIRST SPORTS DAY RACE EVER! THERE'S NO WAY HE CAN WAIT UNTIL NEXT YEAR TO DEFEND HIS TITLE. HE HAS TO BEAT SOMEONE AT SOMETHING – SOON! IT'S TIME FOR SPORTS DAY 2.0...

Do you want to organise your own Sports Day, like Henry? Try playing some of these games against your friends:

1. ~~BEAN BAG~~ TOSS
You will need:

A bean bag

and a bucket

The rules:

Decide on a starting

point to stand and

take turns to

throw the

bean bag into a bucket. Whoever gets it in the most times wins!

2. A RACE

If you're bored of a standard running race, try:

- having a hopping race

- holding a football between your knees for the race

- skipping the race

- balancing a bean bag on your head while running (if you don't have a bean bag, fill a sandwich bag with rice)

3. SKITTLES

You will need:

Skittles (if you don't have skittles, fill a few bottles with some water) and a ball

The rules:

Arrange your skittles together in a group and decide how far away you're going to stand. Take it in turns throwing the ball at the skittles. Whoever knocks the most skittles down wins!

4. OBSTACLE COURSE

You will need: anything!

The rules:

Set up different items and decide how you will interact with them — run around them, jump over them, pick them up and spin around before continuing . . . be creative, then see who can complete the course in the shortest time.

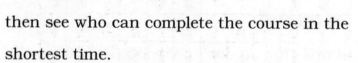

ANSWERS

Identify the Character

A. Perfect Peter B. Horrid Henry C. Moody
Margaret D. Rude Ralph E. Mum F. Miss
Battle-Axe

Wordsearch

K	T	E	D	D	Y	K	F	F	H	Q	S
R	E	K	A	O	S	R	E	P	U	S	E
O	P	T	F	C	O	M	I	C	S	G	B
R	R	B	G	H	F	C	U	O	U	H	U
I	Y	O	Q	L	K	U	W	Q	S	Q	Q
S	C	H	O	C	O	L	A	T	E	W	H
P	X	D	U	F	T	N	D	P	Q	E	K
S	Z	B	L	J	B	S	F	R	J	E	L
V	G	R	V	W	A	K	L	F	L	T	C
U	U	A	P	T	L	U	O	I	S	S	E
D	V	O	W	D	L	E	E	M	M	L	S
N	O	I	S	I	V	E	L	E	T	E	Y

COLLECT ALL THE
HORRID HENRY STORYBOOKS!